Hello, Christmas

By Maryann Cocca-Leffler

cartwheel books™
an imprint of
SCHOLASTIC

Hello, coat,

hello, hood.

Telling Santa

I've been good.

Hello, boxes,

hello, bow.

Singing carols

in the snow.

Hello, cookies, hello, seat.

Family gathers—
oh so sweet.

Hello, sled,

hello, hill.

Cocoa for the winter chill.

Hello, farm,

hello, tree.

Decorate for all to see.

Hello, bed,

hello, light.

Santa will arrive tonight.

Hello, morning, hello, sun.

Hello Christmas,
everyone!

Merry
Christmas!